JUSTICE & LIBERTY
"DO YOU SEE ME?"

Mykah Montgomery

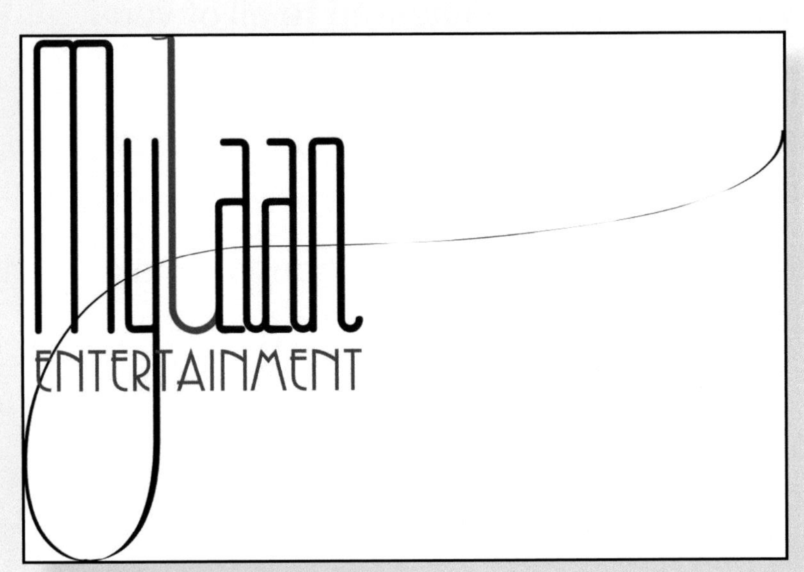
Mylaan
ENTERTAINMENT

MM
Mykah Montgomery

Justice & Liberty "Do you see me?" is dedicated to all of you beautiful children in the world.

No matter what we look like, no matter what others see, we are all the same in God's family.

Be true. Be good. Be kind. Give love all the time. Though it may be hard some days, God knows and will hold your hand and guide you to be the very best you can be.

You are precious in God's sight and in mine too, and you can do whatever "good" you set your mind to.

Always remember that you can do all things through Christ who strengthens you (Philippians 4:13).

With love,

Mykah Montgomery
www.mykahm.com

Mykah Montgomery

Book number 4, Justice and Liberty Do You See Me, is a new addition to the Mykah Montgomery OK2B Different book series - inspiring books that focus on:

#Diversity, Equity & Inclusion
#Loving yourself and others
#Child entrepreneurship

Justice & Liberty "Do you see me?"

Book number 3, Twinzies, is about two young ladies who appear different on the outside, but celebrate and embrace their similarities above all else. “Twinzies are we and Twinzies we’ll be!”

Twinzies

Book number 2, Isaiah Wants to Read, is about an African American boy who loves to read, struggled with dyslexia, and encourages others to find fun and excitement in gaining knowledge and experiencing new adventures while reading. He also becomes a child entrepreneur and believes, as does Millie from The Little Girl Who Wanted a Tail, that he can do all things.

Isaiah Wants to Read

Book number 1, The Little Girl Who Wanted a Tail, and its theme song, is about an African American girl who struggles with being different, but with the love and support of her family and belief that she can do all things, she becomes a confident child entrepreneur.

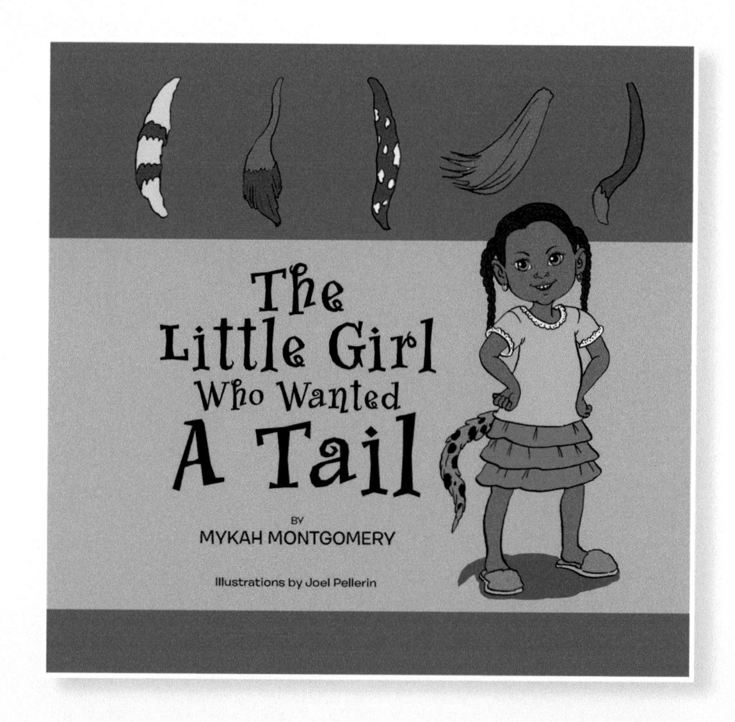

The Little Girl Who Wanted a Tail

LISTEN:
**"Different" http://mykahmontgomery.
bandcamp.com/track/different**

WATCH:
**"Different" music video
http://www.youtube. com/watch?v=irxtMd1TKeg**

TALKBACK:
**Facebook:
https://www.facebook.com/mykahmontgomeryauthor**

**Twitter & Instagram:
https://twitter.com/mykah72author
Instagram - mebooks2023**

AVAILABLE:
**All books in Mykah Montgomery's OK2B Different
book series are available at Xlibris.com**

**https://www.xlibris.com/en/bookstore/
bookdetails/742978-isaiah-wants-to-read**

**https://www.xlibris.com/en/bookstore/
bookdetails/598372-the-little-girl-who-wanted-a-tail**

**https://www.xlibris.com/en/bookstore/
bookdetails/806661-twinzies**

**Also available at www.mykahm.com/author, Amazon.
com, Barnes & Noble.com, And many online retailers.
Search Mykah Montgomery and the book name.**

Illustrated by Ken Hoskin.

To order additional copies of this book, contact:
Xlibris
844-714-8691
www.Xlibris.com
Orders@Xlibris.com

ISBN:	Softcover	978-1-6698-6146-1
	EBook	978-1-6698-6145-4

Print information available on the last page

Rev. date: 01/04/2022

JUSTICE & LIBERTY

"DO YOU SEE ME?"

Millicent's Tail
for Sale
Oh The Tales Tails Tell
MATTER

Do you see me?

I see you.

I see that you can be good

Do you see me the same way? You should.

I want to be loved.

I want respect.

I want to be someone that you truly vow to protect.

Millicent's
for Sale
Oh The Tales Tai
WE MATTER

You smile when you see me.

You stop and say hello.

You are fair and just with everyone, and it shows.

That is how I see you in my mind.

That is how I'd like to see you all the time.

You are a person just like me.

We both feel hurt.

We both feel joy.

Before you grew up, like me, you were just a little boy.

Didn't you run and play?

Didn't you look forward to the next day?

These are things I do.

I bet they are things you did too.

Millicent's Tail-
for Sale
Oh The Tales Tails Tell
WE
MATTER

Do you see me?

I see you.

I see that you can be good.

You see me the same way, right? You should.

Millicent's Tails
for Sale
Oh The Tales Tails Tell
WE MATTER

When I see you I want there to be a smile on your face.

I want you to carry yourself with dignity and grace.

I want to know you care.

You care very much about our community and everyone there.

DST

I know that all people don't do right all the time.

Just because I may look like them, please don't assume their ways are mine.

Give me the freedom to be the great person God created me to be.

Judge me by how *I* act, not the behavior you think you'll see.

Sale
ales Tails Tell
WE MATTER
DST
NCBW 100

We come from different family trees.

Generations of people who lived to be free.

Free to love.

Free to be.

Free to live in a world with justice for all and liberty.

Do you see me?

I see you.

I see that you can be good

Do you see me the same way? I hope so - you should.

LOVE

Yes, I see you.

I know you see me.

I know that you are good.

You have the right to live in peace and harmony.

I promise I'll do my very best, to be the person God created me to be.

To protect and serve you and our community, safely.

I will be just.

I will be fair.

I'll show you that I care.

You deserve love.

You deserve respect.

You deserve to be a special someone that I protect.

Millicent's
for Sale
Oh The Tales Tails
WE MATTER

Thank you young man for taking the time to share with me what's on your mind.

You did it in a kind and loving way.

That is appreciated, I must say.

I look forward to all of us feeling safe, loved, and respected.

I promise to do my part to lead us into that glorious day.

LINKS
DST
LOVE

Thank you officer.

You are welcome, my friend.

The End

Thank you to Leaders are Readers, Inc. for encouraging young people to read and share their own stories.

www.larsinc.org

Thank you, my sorors and sisters from the following organizations:

- Delta Sigma Theta Sorority, Incorporated
- The Links, Incorporated
- National Coalition of 100 Black Women, Incorporated

My family, especially mom, Sylvia Montgomery, dad, David Montgomery, brother, Anthony Montgomery, and daughter, the inspiration for Millie, The Little Girl Who Wanted a Tail, Mylaan Imani Gant. I also thank God for each and every one of my dear friends, supports, and for you.

Printed in the United States
by Baker & Taylor Publisher Services